One day, Doug-Dennis and
Ben-Bobby were bored.

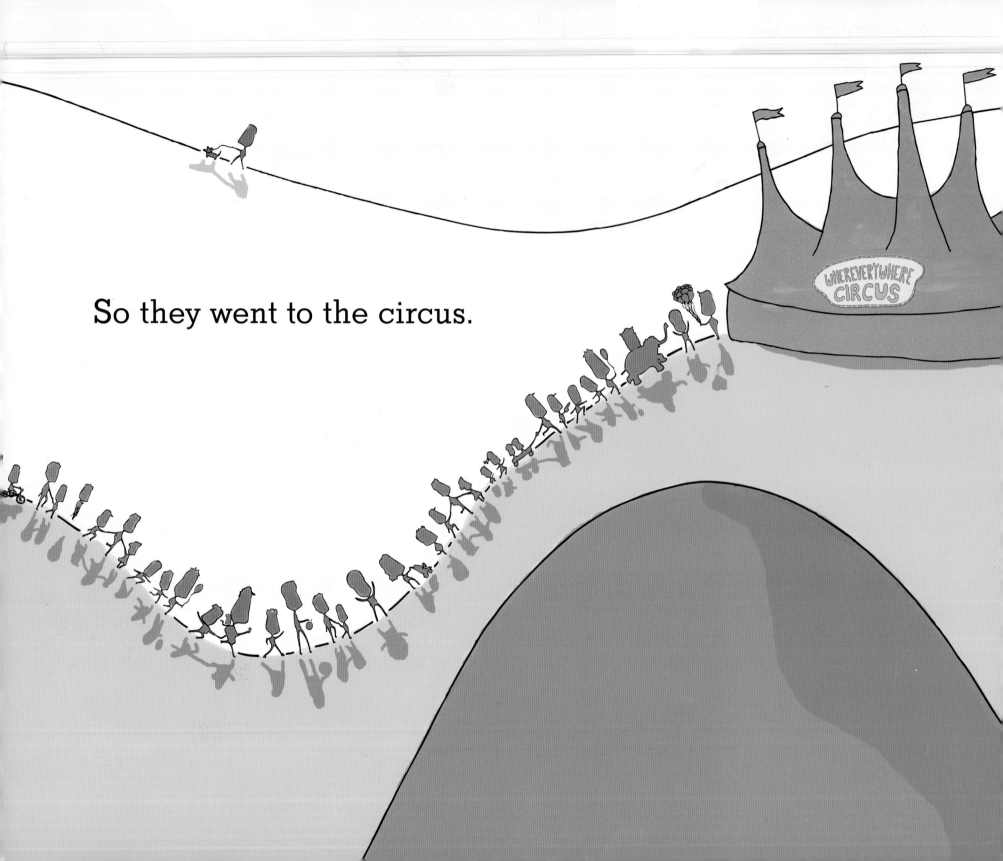

So they went to the circus.

Doug-Dennis
AND THE Flyaway Fib

WORDS AND PICTURES BY

Darren Farrell

DIAL BOOKS FOR YOUNG READERS
an imprint of Penguin Group (USA) Inc.

DIAL BOOKS FOR YOUNG READERS
A division of Penguin Young Readers Group • Published by The Penguin Group Penguin Group (USA) Inc., 375 Hudson Street, New York, NY 10014, U.S.A.
Penguin Group (Canada), 90 Eglinton Avenue East, Suite 700, Toronto, Ontario, Canada M4P 2Y3 (a division of Pearson Penguin Canada Inc.) • Penguin
Books Ltd, 80 Strand, London WC2R 0RL, England • Penguin Ireland, 25 St. Stephen's Green, Dublin 2, Ireland (a division of Penguin Books Ltd)
Penguin Group (Australia), 250 Camberwell Road, Camberwell, Victoria 3124, Australia (a division of Pearson Australia Group Pty Ltd)
Penguin Books India Pvt Ltd, 11 Community Centre, Panchsheel Park, New Delhi - 110 017, India • Penguin Group (NZ),
67 Apollo Drive, Rosedale, North Shore 0632, New Zealand (a division of Pearson New Zealand Ltd)
Penguin Books (South Africa) (Pty) Ltd, 24 Sturdee Avenue, Rosebank, Johannesburg 2196, South Africa
Penguin Books Ltd, Registered Offices: 80 Strand, London WC2R 0RL, England

Designed by Jennifer Kelly
Text set in Stymie

Manufactured in China on acid-free paper

10 9 8 7 6 5 4 3 2 1

Library of Congress Cataloging-in-Publication Data
Farrell, Darren.
Doug-Dennis and the flyaway fib/words and pictures by Darren Farrell.
p. cm.
Summary: Having fibbed about stealing his best friend's popcorn at the circus, Doug-Dennis the sheep finds himself carried far away
to a place filled with lies and liars of all sorts and must discover a way to return.
ISBN 978-0-8037-3437-1 (hardcover)
[1. Honesty—Fiction. 2. Best friends—Fiction. 3. Friendship—Fiction. 4. Circus—Fiction. 5. Sheep—Fiction.] I. Title.
PZ7.F2445Dou 2010
[E]—dc22
2009012141

This book was created with pen and ink
and Photoshop and Illustrator and iced coffee
and not enough sleep.

POP CORN

But before they
could have any
fun at all...

Doug-Dennis
did something
dreadful.

He told a fib.

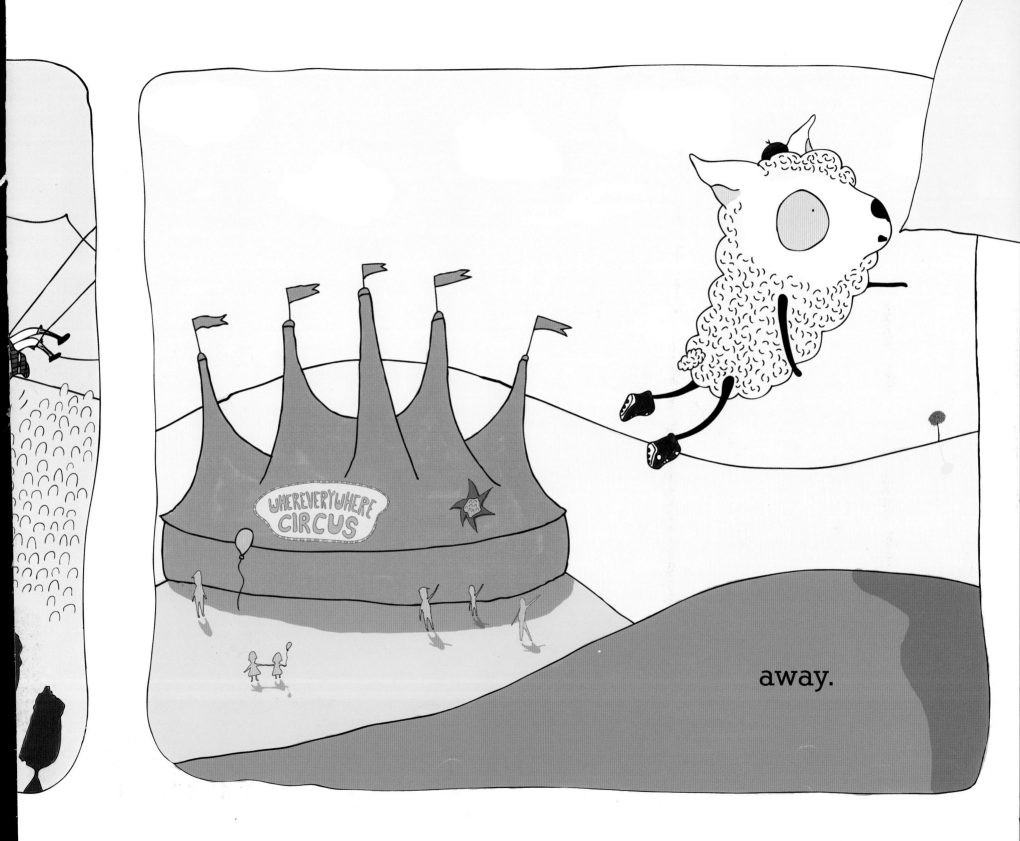

away.

"AND IF I WERE A BAZILLIONAIRE, I WOULD TOTALLY BUY YOU A NEW TUB OF POPCORN, BEN-BOBBY. BEN-BOBBY!!?"

When he was frightfully high in the dark night sky and terribly far from home...

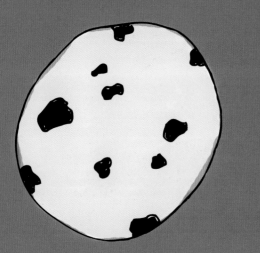

and the truth had stretched as far
as truth will stretch and the fib was
now a BIG FAT LIE...

Doug-Dennis saw something
few boys ever see.

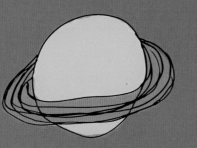

There in the air everywhere he looked…

I CAN FLY!!!
NO SERIOUSLY, I'M A FLYING SQUIRREL. I SWEAR.

I DIDN'T BURP! THAT WAS MY INVISIBLE FRIEND ROBERT.

were people of all shapes and sizes…

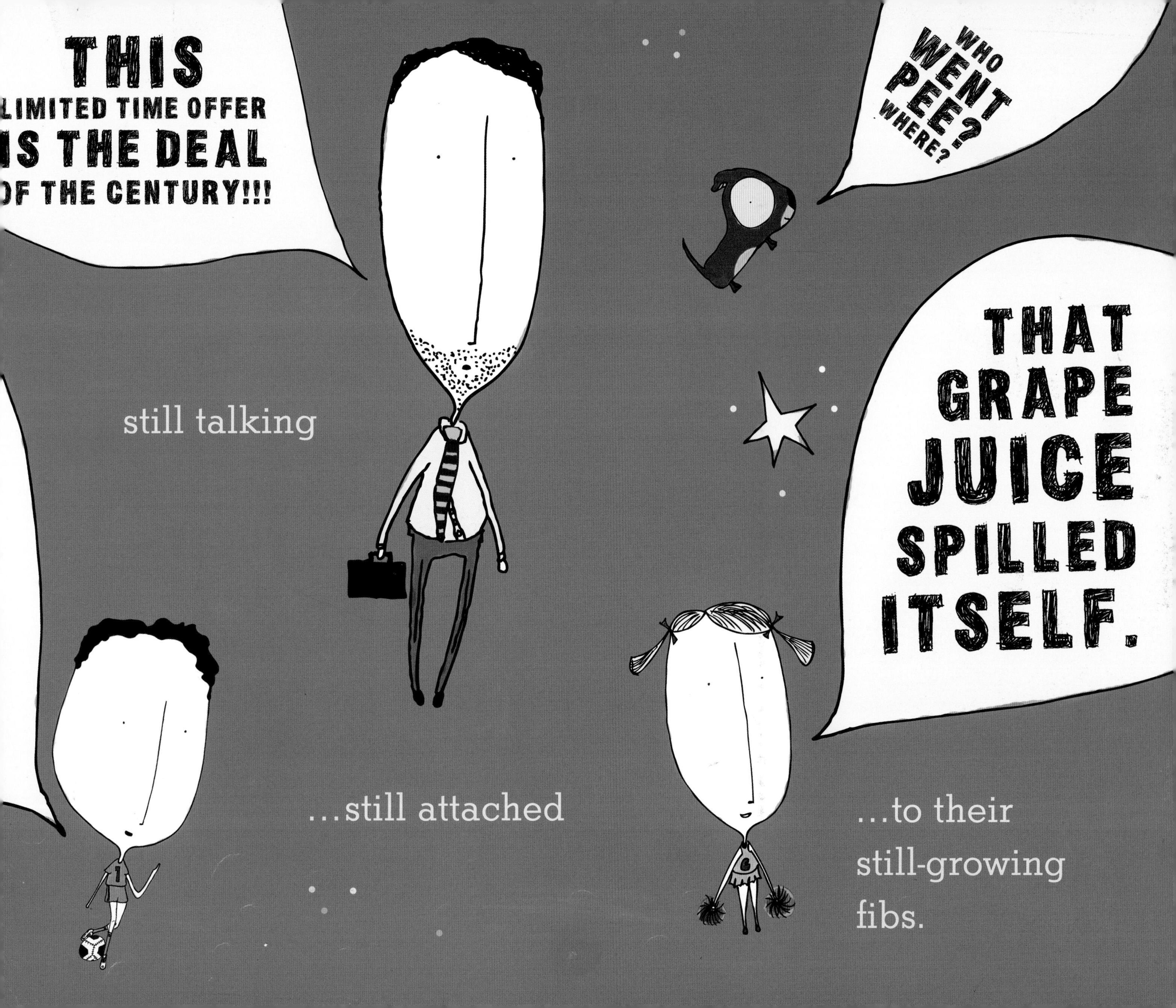

still talking

. . . still attached

. . . to their still-growing fibs.

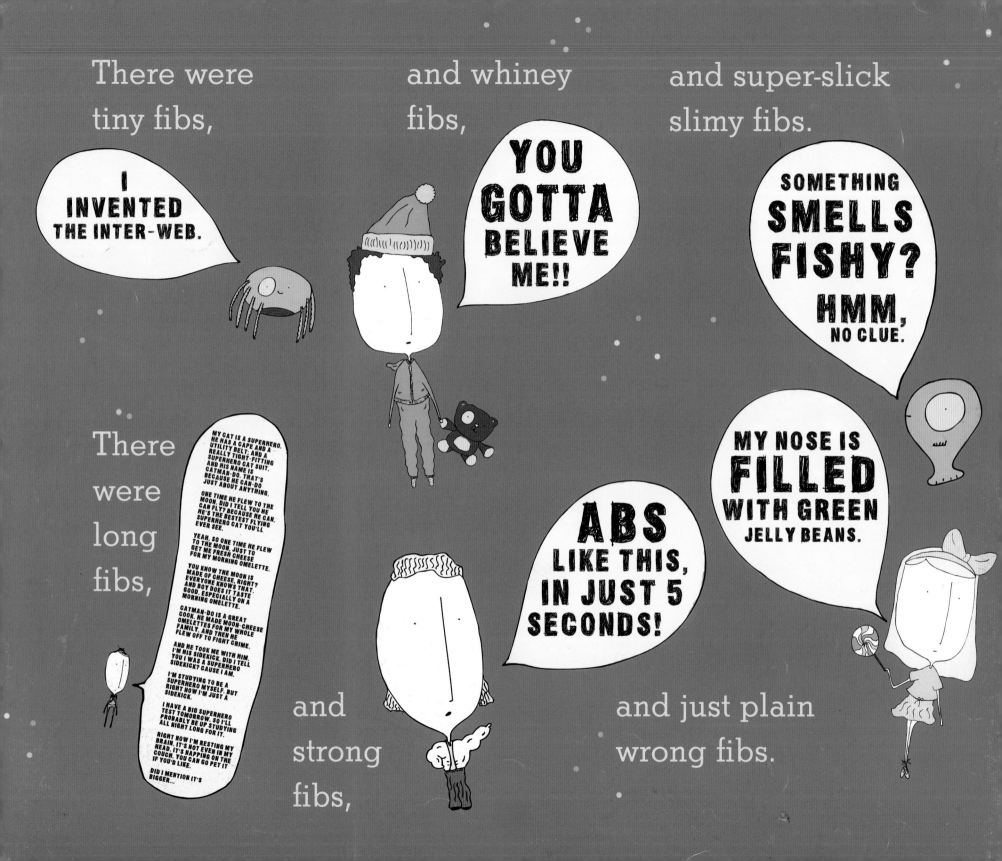

SERIOUSLY,
THE DOG
ATE MY
HOMEWORK.

HE
DID IT.

Some fibs had been
up there for a VERY
long time...

SOMEONE
HELP!
MONSTERS ATE
MY BEST FRIEND'S
POPCORN.

while others
had just
arrived.

BLAH
BLAH
BLAH

H
AH
AH
H

Doug-Dennis couldn't believe
his ears. Everyone spoke at
once and no one listened to
anything anyone else said.

BLAH
BLAH

BLAH

Doug-Dennis was sad. He wished he hadn't tricked his best friend. He wished he had told the truth.

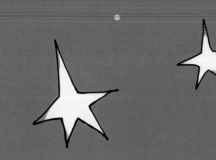

So that is exactly what
Doug-Dennis did.

INCREDIBLY DELICIOUS POPCORN! I DID.

And Doug-Dennis sailed swiftly back toward the circus.

He landed with a thud right back where the fib began. Then Doug-Dennis finally told his best friend the truth.

And with that, Doug-Dennis
never ever fibbed again.